Kiss Kiss!

Margaret Wild & Bridget Strevens-Marzo

SIMON & SCHUSTER BOOKS FOR YOUNG READERS

New York   London   Toronto   Sydney   Singapore

One day when Baby Hippo woke up,
he was in such a rush to go and play that he
forgot to give his mama a kiss.

"Oh!" said Mama.

Through the squelchy, squelchy mud waddled Baby Hippo.
And this is what he heard . . .

"Kiss, kiss!"

Around the bumpy, bumpy rocks waddled Baby Hippo.
And this is what he heard . . .

"Kiss, kiss!"

Up the mossy, mossy bank waddled Baby Hippo.
And this is what he heard . . .

"Kiss, kiss!"

Through the long, long grass waddled Baby Hippo.
And this is what he heard . . .

"Kiss, kiss!"

Under the leafy, leafy trees waddled Baby Hippo.
And this is what he heard . . .

"Kiss, kiss!"

Baby Hippo stopped. He suddenly remembered
something he'd forgotten to do.

Baby Hippo hurried back under the leafy, leafy trees,

through the long, long grass,

down the mossy, mossy bank,

around the bumpy, bumpy rocks,

through the squelchy, squelchy mud, to find his mama.

But he couldn't see his mama anywhere.
"Oh!" said Baby Hippo.

Then out of the deep, deep water appeared two eyes,
two wiggling ears, and a pair of snorting nostrils.
"Peekaboo!" said Mama.

Baby Hippo beamed.
"Kiss, kiss?" he said.
"Kiss, *kiss!*" said Mama.

For Karen and Olivia—M. W.

For Ella—B. S.-M.

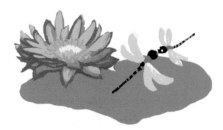

SIMON & SCHUSTER BOOKS FOR YOUNG READERS

An imprint of Simon & Schuster Children's Publishing Division

1230 Avenue of the Americas, New York, New York 10020

Text copyright © 2003 by Margaret Wild

Illustrations copyright © 2003 by Bridget Strevens-Marzo

First published in Australia in 2003 by Little Hare Books.

First U.S. edition 2004

SIMON & SCHUSTER BOOKS FOR YOUNG READERS is a trademark of Simon & Schuster.

Book design by ANTART

The text for this book is set in Lemonade.

Manufactured in Hong Kong

10 9 8 7 6 5 4 3 2 1
Library of Congress Cataloging-in-Publication Data
Wild, Margaret, 1948-
Kiss kiss / Margaret Wild ; illustrated by Bridget Strevens-Marzo.—1st U.S. ed.
p. cm.
Summary: Baby Hippo is in such a rush to play one morning he forgets to kiss his mama, but
strangely all the jungle noises seem to remind him.
ISBN 0-689-86279-2 (Hardcover)
[1. Hippopotamus—Fiction. 2. Mother and child—Fiction. 3.
Kissing—Fiction.] I. Strevens-Marzo, Bridget, ill. II. Title.
PZ7.W64574Ki 2004
[E]—dc21   2002154516